The Stranger Who Smiled

Hunter Jones

ISBN-13: **978-0-578-46784-9**

DEDICATION

This book is dedicated to every person who assisted in the process of creating this book. To list a few: Raylee. Skyla, Daya, and Twin #2. There were many more, but these four were so dedicated to keeping the process moving. They fell in love with the story just as much as I did, while creating theories about what could possibly come next!

Thank you!

CONTENTS

PROLOGUE

Alderton was a small unassuming town where nothing much out of the ordinary happened. The kind of town where everyone knew everybody and their business. A young man named David lived here with his younger brother Conner, who was an avid artist at the age of 13. The boys lived in a small faint yellow house next to the town's bookstore which was the teenage hangout after hours. Conner often would go to the bookstore to hang out with his friends but he would still check in with David from time to time to let him know he was alright. This week was the first week of August, the beginnings of Autumn. Conner was soon to be 14, with his birthday on the 3rd. The night of August 1st Conner is staying with his friend, Matthew, to celebrate his upcoming birthday.

1 THE SEARCH FOR A GIFT

David was sitting silently reading one of his favorite books from his childhood, when all of the sudden the door burst open. Conner ran through the living room and straight to his bedroom. "What the heck are you doing back here?" David called after him. Conner, breathing heavily, walked back into the living room. "Aren't you at Matthew's tonight?" Conner held up a white cord to show David.

"I forgot my charger, Matthew doesn't have this kind and I didn't want my phone to die," Conner said hastily. He started to walk out the door to head down the street when he paused and remembered something. "Don't forget my birthday is coming up, you better get me something good!" He proclaimed. David waved the thought away and said goodbye to Conner.

As the door clicked shut David quickly set down his book and pulled out his laptop. "What on earth am I gonna do?" David questioned as he opened Google and typed in *What to get a 13 year old for his birthday* "He surely wouldn't want another set of paint brushes," he said to Melody, their 7 year old grey tabby. The cat only twitched an ear in response.

"What a great help you are," David said sarcastically. He closed the laptop rather aggressively and groaned out of frustration, he couldn't find anything helpful on the internet. Deciding to take a stroll across town to see if he could find any inspiration, he stepped out the doo2 | P a g e r and took a deep breath. It was rather cold today so he stepped back inside to grab a jacket.

"Alright Melody, hold the fort down, I'm headed out to find a gift for Conner," he said to the cat who yawned and stretched. He closed the door then took off down the driveway and onto the sidewalk.

He looked over to the bookstore and thought that'd be a good place to start. David loved books more than anything, maybe he could get Conner a book on art. As he walked up, the doors slid open and he was met with a familiar face. The bookkeeper, James was a well-built man who was 25 years old, just three years older than David. He wore glasses and had a closely trimmed beard.

"Mr. Walker, nice to see you back again." James said with a smile. David turned red because he admired James and got nervous whenever they spoke.

"Mr. Haul, how is your day going?" David stuttered.

"It's going great, been a bit slow today, with all the teens over at Matthew's tonight for Conner's birthday. What are you up to?" James asked.

"Not much, I was just looking for something to get Conner for his birthday this year. where are the art books?" David questioned. James pointed to a shelf towards the back corner on the left. David thanked him and headed over to the corner. The books were neatly lined up on the shelf in alphabetical order by author. David ran his fingers across their spines as he read the titles.

"Darn it, nothing good." David sighed, "Oh well, maybe I'll ask James to get coffee, he could possibly have some thoughts on what to get him." David pulled out a book and skimmed through it, thinking about his idea. He turned red at the thought then closed the book and groaned. " I would never be able to ask James to get coffee, what if…"

"I say no?" Said a voice from behind the bookshelf. David jumped and dropped the book he was holding.

"Crap, I was thinking out loud again," David stuttered to himself as he fumbled for the book. James walked around the bookshelf and stood in front of David.

"Yep, and I enjoy coffee. I don't see why I wouldn't go with you. It's a reasonable thing to ask someone for assistance," James smiled, "plus I think it would be nice to have coffee with you." David awkwardly put the book back on the shelf, almost dropping it again. James let out a small laugh. "So I'll meet you there at 6? After my shift is over." David agreed and headed back home.

He opened the door and took a step inside, then closed the door forcefully. Melody perked her ears up and looked at David questioningly. David leaned against the door and put his hands over his face, trying to hide his embarrassment. Melody sauntered over and pawed at his leg, she was hungry. He picked up the cat and let out a big sigh.

"Oh Mel, what have I gotten myself into? I've never been on an actual date before what if I mess it up?" The cat meowed in response. David sat her down, went to the kitchen, grabbed her food, then filled her bowl. "It's in two hours, what should I do? I am definitely not ready!" Melody ran to her food and took a few bites then looked up at David and let out a small "mew" then continued eating. "You're right, it's not actually a date, he is only helping me come up with gift ideas." David took a deep breath, then went to take a shower.

As David finished the last touches on his outfit, he went to the bathroom to fix his hair and brush his teeth, his alarm went off. It was 5:30, it was time for him to get to the coffee shop on the other side to town. He quickly finished combing his hair and turned out the lights. He had left in such a hurry that he hadn't noticed the sounds coming from the back yard, nor had he noticed his back door creaking open. He started up his truck and headed out. David was always early, it didn't matter if it had been his own funeral, he would have been early by thirty minutes.

David pulled into the parking spot in front of the coffee shop and put his truck in park. Locking the truck up, he noticed something out of the ordinary. Mr. and Mrs. Sheffield haven't left the coffee shop to head home, they usually leave by four. David walked inside and sat his bag down on the table just to the right of the doors. He sat down and decided to listen in on what they were saying.

"Scott, you have to help us! Wellington has gone missing and I'm absolutely sure it has something to do with that stranger that waltzed into town the other day!" Mr. Sheffield insisted. His wife pulled out a cloth and dabbed her tears away. These two were always causing trouble and blowing stuff out of proportion, especially when their dog, Wellington, was involved. Scott Reynolds was the town sheriff and he always listened to everyone, no matter how dull or bizarre the issue. David sat up straight when he heard about the stranger though, how come he hadn't noticed before? A visitor in Alderton was rare; last time a visitor came through, they caused a whole lot of trouble. The town never really trusted strangers because of this.

He decided to let the thought pass as he noticed James pull up into a parking spot. It was 6:00, David became really excited and wanted to run up to greet him but he just sat in his spot and waved as James walked through the door.

"Good afternoon David!" James said happily.

"Hey James, have you heard the news?" Asked David as James came to sit down.

"Not anything that's out of the ordinary, why?" James said.

"Well, apparently the Sheffields' dog has gone missing and there is a stranger in town." David replied.

"Well that is a bit odd, do you think the stranger had something to do with Wellington?" James asked. David laughed a little.

"I honestly don't care about the dog, he likes to tear up my garden whenever he gets out. I'm sure he is just sniffing about in the eastern woods." David scoffed. James agreed and they both had a little laugh.

"I'll be back in one second, the drive here made me parched," James said jokingly as he got up and went to order some coffee for the two of them. He made sure to order David tea because he knew that he wasn't a fan of coffee. The barista called out James's name and he grabbed the drinks then came back with a sly smile on his face.

"Oh? What did you get me?" Asked David, raising an eyebrow.

"Take a sip and find out, I bet you won't hate it." James said with a smile and a quick wink. David decided to test it and see if he would survive this encounter with coffee; he lifted the cup and took a sip, to his surprise it was not coffee, but it was tea.

"You remembered? Thank you, it was very kind of you to get me a drink." David smiled lightly at the thought of James remembering that he didn't like coffee.

"Of course! Now enough about us, we need to think of something for Conner." James said changing the subject.

"Oh right, I almost forgot…" David said trailing off with embarrassment.

"Well, what does Conner like to do in his spare time?" Asked James.

To which David replied frustratingly. "He likes art, but I get him stuff for that every time I need a gift for him." James hummed to himself as he thought of what else there could be.

After an hour of talking and thinking about gift ideas, the two decided it was getting late. "Well this has been great but I have got to head home soon, I haven't eaten all day." James announced patting his stomach, as if to show how empty it was. It was now 7:00 and Alderton started to wind down around 7:30, as most small towns do. Then the two got up and walked out the door.

"I'll walk you to your truck at least." James said as they they started to head towards David's little white truck.

"Thank you for tonight, it's been great." David said in a small voice as they arrived at the truck.

"It's been wonderful David. Next time you will have to let me take you to dinner in the next town over, I hear they have a good burger place." James said as he leaned against the door of David's truck.

David turned red then looked at the ground and smiled shyly. "I'd love that, thank you again for helping me with his gift." David said. Then, as he reached for the door handle, James intercepted for a hug. David was surprised but as James hugged him, he felt like his stress disappeared and the world froze for a moment. James pulled away and smiled at David.

"Goodnight, I'll see you soon at the shop right?" James asked to which David replied with a nod and a smile, he was too stunned to actually respond. David hopped in his truck as James walked back to his vehicle. He then took a deep breath, smiled a big smile, and drove back home.

2 MISSING PETS

David parked his truck in the driveway and headed inside. As he closed the door and stepped into the living room, he listened closely, it was silent. There was no cat that came up meowing to greet him.

"Melody?" David called out only to have silence in response. He walked into the kitchen to see if she had hidden in there. To no surprise, the cat was not there either. Instead the back door was cracked open and the faint whistle of wind could be heard. David pulled the door open and peeked out into the back yard. All he could see was the single cherry tree sitting in the now dimming daylight.

"I'll have to search for her tomorrow," he sighed to himself, then right as he went to close the door he looked past his and his neighbor's yard to see a dark figure standing in the shadows. It looked to be holding something that was squirming. The faint light that was shining on the side of this figure lit up part of his face, which was twisted into an eerie smile that gave David the chills. He heard a knock at front door and nearly jumped out of his skin. When he looked back the figure was gone, so he waved it away as a figment of his own imagination and closed the door. He shuffled his way back into the living room and to the front door. The knock hit again and sounded urgent, so David opened the door interrupting the knock.

David was nearly knocked in the face by his neighbor, Kaitlyn Lambers, who was a short blonde girl that just turned twenty years old. "Kaitlyn? What's the matter?" He asked noticing that she looked very upset. She barged inside and sat on the couch looking at her hands, obviously disoriented.

"I don't know how it happened! One moment I was opening a cabinet and the next I turn around and see something in my backyard! I opened the door and he was gone!" She let out in a cacophony of sobs and half formed words.

"Woah, slow down. I can't understand you, who was gone? What did you see?" David said as he sat down next to the distressed girl trying to console her. Kaitlyn took a big breath and slowly let it out.

Finally she had calmed down enough to speak normally. "I was about to let Brutus in and feed him. So I went to the cabinet to get his food, I opened it then set it down on the counter because I heard a noise." She had explained.

"What kind of noise did you hear?" David questioned as he grew concerned.

"It was a sort of a thump then a clank followed by a shriek that was not human. I went to look out the window, I was worried for my dog, and instead of my dog I saw this... thing. It was horrible. It had a hunched back and it's arms were long and lanky but looked twisted. It didn't see me until I noticed that the chain that I had my dog on, was snapped and I let out a small squeal and it turned around to face me. That's when I saw it's face..." she trailed off looking at the wall, she was staring into a memory and was horrified by what she saw. She continued but in a very small voice, starting to sob again, and stuttered out "...It looked like a-a-a human face? B-b-but with a very thin and wide s-s-s-smile." David looked through the doorway out the kitchen window and thought to himself about the figure that he saw on the street over.

She drifted back into focus looking a bit more serious. She asked David if she could stay with him for a few nights because she lived alone. "Absolutely, I'd probably be scared to be alone as well. You are welcome to the spare bedroom, it hasn't got any windows so if you leave the light off, it can be hard to keep track of time." David said with a light hearted smile. She hugged him and said her thanks as he led her to the spare.

"Also can I ask that you don't tell anyone? They will think I'm insane and send me off to the Blue Hearth." She pleaded.

"My lips are sealed, it won't leave this house." David had replied pretending to lock his lips and throw away the key.

He had known Kaitlyn for quite a while and they were good friends. He knew that something weird must've happened to get her this scared. She had loved creepy stuff and not much scared her these days, but she was mortified. David went back to the kitchen and grabbed his phone off the counter, made sure all the doors were locked, and the lights turned off. Once this was completed he headed back to his room and plopped down onto his bed. He opened his phone and dialed in his brother's number.

After the third ring, Conner finally picked up. "Hey Conner, how is your night going?" asked David.

"It's great, we were supposed to play with Matthew's dogs, but they have gone missing," replied Conner. David almost dropped his phone at this comment. He sat up and looked out the window. That's why it's quiet! All the pets have gone missing! How could this have happened? David thought about that figure again. "Hello?"

David forgot that he was on the phone. "Yeah, sorry. I got distracted. Hey stay inside tonight and make sure the doors are locked okay?" David sounded a bit rigid when he said this. Conner knew something was wrong so he agreed and said goodnight. David set his phone down on the bedside table and laid back down on his bed. Lying supine, he stared at the ceiling.

He stayed up all night thinking about that figure, it gave him the chills. What if it had been the one to take the animals? Was there more than one? Would it move on to things other than pets? What is it going to do with the pets? Will the pets ever be seen again? He eventually drifted off to sleep still thinking about all of the unanswered questions that will haunt his dreams.

3 THE NIGHTMARE

That night he dreamt of the events that day but the memories were twisted and wrong. He was sitting on his couch reading his book, but instead of it being his book, it was bound with skin. He couldn't read the words because they were in some ancient language. David heard the door creak open and in walked his brother, his posture was poor and he hid his face. David asked him what he was doing and Conner flinched at his voice. David sounded angry and shouted at Conner to look at him. Conner slowly lifted his head to face David. His eyes were dazed and had a white film over them. David could feel himself starting to grin at the sight. He studied Conner and his smile was wiped off his face when he noticed that Conner wasn't smiling. David became enraged, he grabbed Conner and threw him onto the coffee table holding him down. Conner did little to fight back knowing that it would only make David's anger worse. David pulled out a knife from his back pocket and squeezed the hilt giddily. Conner, being pinned to the table, made no sounds but let out a single tear from his left eye. David laughed and put the knife right up to Conner's cheek, catching his tear. He then licked the blade of his knife and looked at his brother hard.

"You must be happy and smile!" David could hear himself say in a tone that would give anyone the chills. He brought the knife up to his brothers lips and traced out a thin yet long line across Conner's face, forming what would be a messed up grin.

He then yelled at Conner to smile, in response he attempted to grin as large as he could, while tears started streaming down his face at an increasing rate. David then took the knife and put it at the corner of Conner's mouth, laughing gleefully as he did so. He started to cut at Conner's mouth tracing that same line he followed a second ago. Conner didn't scream out of fear that he would only anger David more than he already was. As David finished slicing the right side, he moved to the left side to copy the cut. Conner's tears now mixed with the blood that leaked from his mouth that will forever be smiling. David finished the left side and stood back to look at his piece of art he just created.

"Sit up!" David shouted. Conner slowly sat up on the coffee table, he tilted his head and stared hazily through David. Blood ran from his grin down onto his clothes and drenched them. David then ripped a phone charger out of the wall and slammed it hard into Conner's chest.

"I had better not see you again tonight." David said in a harsh tone. Conner then stood up letting the charger drag on the ground. He pulled open the door and left, dragging his feet along the ground as he walked.

David, now covered in his brother's blood, walked out the door and looked down the street. He smiled when he saw the bookstore, which was closed and empty except for the clerk. He walked up to the door and tapped on it with his knife. James came to the door and unlocked it, letting David in. James was absurdly tall and extremely thin; he looked as though he hadn't had a meal for weeks. David walked past him and straight to the back, where there was a shelf of peculiar looking books. The books resembled the one he had been reading earlier. He ran his finger along their spines reading their names as he came across them, though they were not any language he knew. He pulled one out and flipped through its pages resting on a page that looked like a sort of recipe. It had a picture of a creature coming out of the ground as if it was being birthed from the underworld. David smiled and knew that he had to be the one to make this thing happen. He ripped the page out and stuffed it into his pocket then walked out after whispering something to James.

The dream went blurry and when it came back into focus he was at the coffee shop and he was sitting alone at a table. The shop was empty, with the exception of some bodies lying about and the barista. Mr. Sheffield's body had looked like he was ripped in half by a bear, his left side slouching much lower in his chair than his right half. Mrs. Sheffield's body sat across from him, though her head was ripped off of her body and was now resting on Mr. Sheffield's plate. The town sheriff was also there but his body was laying on the table, his gun was in his hand and on the top of his head you could see through a bullet hole into his mouth. The shop was a bloodied mess, but to David this felt completely normal, calming even. The barista was washing some cups with a bloody cloth until a click had been heard, the door had been opened.

The barista suddenly looked terrified, she set down the cup and cloth then backed away slowly, quaking with fear. At the door, a figure appeared and walked towards David. Before the figure sat down at the table, David took the page out of his pocket and slid the paper to the other side of the table. The figure then sat down opposite David, it was someone he had never seen before, a stranger. The stranger had an overcoat on and a hat with a large brim so that you couldn't see his face very well, all you could see was his mouth. The stranger reached out with his long twisted arms and grabbed the paper, he let out a low gravelly sounding laugh that would chill anyone to the bone. Then he smiled, the corners of his mouth almost reached from ear to ear. His smile was thin and chilling, his teeth were yellowing with age and he had drool dripping from his mouth as if he were starving and a pie was just placed in front of him. David smiled then stood up to leave, his job had been done. The Paper was delivered and the creature would be born into the world.

The world went dark as David could hear the sound of knocking at the front door. He had woken up from that nightmare of a world. His bed was soaked, as was he, David had been sweating all night long. He felt as if he couldn't breathe, his breaths were short and heavy. The knock at the door was louder this time.

"Hold on, I'm coming!" David yelled out in reply. He climbed out of bed and started towards the door. Opening the door he was greeted with an angry brother.

"I've been knocking for ten minutes, your phone was off!"
Conner said haughtily. David reached for his phone in his pocket
only to realize he left it on the table by his bed.

"What time is it?" He asked.

"It's noon, are you okay? You were supposed to pick me up
an hour ago." Conner replied, realizing his brother looked
unhealthy.

"I'm fine, I just had a nightmare. Kaitlyn is staying with us
for a few days, gas leak or something." David said still out of
breath from his nightmare.

They walked inside and Conner sat down on the couch.
"What do you want for breakfast?" David asked.

"It's noon. I'll have a PBJ." Conner answered. David went
into the kitchen and opened the cabinets to get stuff for a peanut
butter and jelly sandwich. Kaitlyn walked into the living room and
sat on the couch next to Conner.

"Man, I had the strangest dream last night." She
announced, David pondered what her dream could have been, he
had quite the dream himself.

4 THE BLACKBERRY BUSH

As evening rolls around, David tells Conner of Melody's disappearance; They decide to go on a search for the gray tabby. Kaitlyn wanted to come along, as she was still freaked out to be alone. The three set off in David's truck and headed towards the edge of town where there was a line of trees that began a small forest.

"This usually ends up being where Melody goes when she gets out, it's her favorite spot." David announced as he turned the keys so the engine died away in a splutter. They all climbed out of the truck and started off in three different directions. David went straight towards the trees, Kaitlyn stuck near the truck, and Conner went to look around the nearby park where there were ball fields and playground equipment.

David got to the edge of forest and started to look close to the ground and in the shrubs. He hopped over the bent down wire fence and walked further into the foliage. To his left was a tall blackberry bush, it was as tall as he was and about eight foot wide. The brambles on the bottom were open revealing a small hole just big enough for a man to crawl through on his stomach.

"That's weird, I don't ever remember a blackberry bush being here," he said aloud to himself. David then squatted down to look at the hole more closely, he thought about how Melody loved to hide in small places, as most cats do. David pulled out his phone and turned the flashlight on and aimed it inside of the hole.

The hole opened up to a sort of cave like area where the walls were the branches of this bush. He decided that he wanted a closer look, it looked like a cool clubhouse of sorts and he likes to explore. David was then lying on his belly and inching forward through this tiny hole filled with thorns.

"Ergh! Ow! Umph...ugh that was a struggle." David said breathing heavily as he finally squirmed through the thorny entrance. He picked up his phone off the ground, as it had fallen out while crawling through. The light on his phone was off,

"Weird, I must've hit it and turned it off by accident," he mumbled to himself as he fumbled to turn it back on. To his surprise his phone was completely off and would not turn on. David grunted and decided to put it in his pocket so he could explore.

The room was very dark and he could barely make out anything other than the stuff just inches from his face. He stretched his arms out and inched towards the edge so he could run his hand along the walls made of brambles. The only light he could see was the small amount that was let in through the small entrance he had come through. He looked back at the darkness and he could see the faint outline of something on the other side of the room. David quickly stiffened; he could be inside of something's den. He held his breath and tried to listen really close to see if he could hear any breathing.

Nothing.

The outline was completely still and lifeless, to this David let out a sigh of relief. But the question still remains, "what is it?" David whispered to himself. He decided to take a closer look and find out for himself. Inching closer, he suddenly felt very anxious and trapped. This was a strange thing for him because he loved to explore and had a strong sense of adventure. The closer he got, the faster his heart would race and sweat started to bead up on his forehead. He got close enough to where he could almost make out a few details but before he could make out what it was he heard a twig snap over by the entrance. He jumped back in surprise and quickly looked for the source of the noise. He saw the light, by the entrance, fading from the daylight melting away.

"How long have I been in here? It should still be bright out for another hour," he said as he laid down to start crawling out of the hole. After a few minutes of struggling and getting scraped up, David finally made it out of the hole.

"David!?" Conner yelled "Where have you been?! Kaitlyn I found him!" Conner yelled out to her. David stood up, he was very confused.

"What do you mean where have I been, I was just checking out this blackberry bush, I went in only five minutes ago." David explained. Kaitlyn ran over from behind a few trees. As David was brushing off his clothes Kaitlyn ran up and kissed him on the mouth. David reeled back in surprise.

"What was that for? You know I'm gay…" David stuttered out.

"Oh shut up, I was worried about you. We had that fight and when you ran off and didn't show up for dinner I was worried." Kaitlyn explained.

"What argument? What is going on?" He asked, getting more and more worried.

"I missed my football kickoff because we went searching for you, what happened?" Conner questioned.

"You don't play football and you aren't supposed to kiss me or make me dinner..." David started getting a bit freaked out. The world started to tilt and spin. His vision started to blur and he put his hands on his head trying to regain his steadiness, But as the world blurred, his legs couldn't hold him anymore and he was now lying on the ground staring at the darkening sky. As he was blacking out he could hear the words of his brother and 'girlfriend' fading in and out.

"Are you alright?"

"What do we do? Carry him?"

"I think he needs a hospital."

"Mom is gonna be upset..."

As he heard the last comment by his brother he accepted his insanity and let the world go dark, with only one thought left on his mind.

Mom?

5 STRANGE WORLD

David was lying down on what felt like a bed, not his own bed, it was smaller and he just barely fit into it. He tried to open his eyes but when he did all he saw was darkness. His heart started to race as he remembered the events of the previous day. Was it even a day ago? How long had he been asleep? He heard the sound of footsteps as he sat up and quickly laid back down, pretending to be asleep. David heard the footsteps stop in front of what seemed like just outside of the room he was in. Petrified, David started to panic, his heart was racing as if it were on its third pot of coffee. He listened hard, wanting to know if they were going to enter the room or not.

Another set of footsteps could be heard coming to meet the first set. The footsteps halted a bit further than the first set, then a voice could be heard. The voice was a gruff sounding man, who seemed very irritated. "When did he stop taking his pills?" he asked. The next voice that he could hear was a voice that he hadn't heard in years, not since her last piano concert.

David knew she had been stressed that day and the doctors said her heart couldn't take stress. She was playing Beethoven's Silence when it happened, halfway through she just froze grabbing at her chest then gasping for air as she fell off of her bench. The crowd all gasped and covered their faces as she lay on the stage turning red in pain as she cried for help. David sat stunned in his seat at the back, then as he realized what was happening he leapt up and ran to the stage as fast as he could. She had stopped breathing by the time he had gotten to her and three other stagehands had already been trying to help her. He tried pushing them away, as he wanted to help her in any way possible. Sirens could be heard as he held her in his arms, crying as only one word repeatedly left his mouth.

Mom.

Her voice was soft yet rigid and strong. "As far as I knew, he had not stopped taking them." She replied in confidence.

"Ms. Walker, this would not have happened had he been taking them on schedule." the man replied sternly. David laid there, stunned beyond what words could describe. It was his mother, she was there and fully alive. "Okay, enough of that, the past is over now. I'm going to see if he has woken up yet." The male voice announced.

The door handle could be heard turning and the door creaked open. David pretended to be asleep and would pretend to have just woken up when they check to see. He could hear the click of a light switch and then it was bright and you could hear the soft humming of the lights overhead. He listened as the footsteps neared the side of his bed then he opened his eyes slowly and pretended to be groggy from sleep.

"Where am I?" David asked as his vision focused to the new light level. Standing by his bed was a short man who had blond hair and wore thick glasses. On his white overcoat, a nametag read the man's last name, Flanigan. Dr. Flanigan was the town's quack doctor, it's who you went to if you were thought to have gone insane.

"The Blue Hearth Clinic," He said with a soft tone. This was the name of the shrink's office, if someone ended up here then they usually get shipped off to an asylum or something. "You come here once a week, remember?"

"What? I've never been here before, this is where they send the crazy people." David retorted, getting a bit frustrated. David heard a noise from the door, then he froze as he remembered that his mother was here. She took a step into the room and looked at him with a face filled with sorrow.

"David…" She said as her eyes started to tear up "you say this every time we come here, it's always the same story too."

"Mom? I…I missed you but you should be…"

"Dead, we know." Flanigan interrupted becoming impatient. "This time, as I have informed your mother, we are keeping you here until you are ready to leave for sure."

David's mom started to sob due to her son's deteriorating mind. David stopped listening to what was being said and began staring off at the wall trying to make sense of what is happening. He snapped out of it, remembering his brother. "What day is it today?" He asked hoping it hadn't been more than a day. His heart sank as he heard the date.

"August 4th, you missed Conner's birthday." His mother replied through a tissue that was being used to wipe her makeup to keep it from running. He thought about his brother, he had been Conner's anchor for years, he watched after him ever since that day. For some unknown reason David thought back to his dream, the look on his brother's face when he first walked in. He shuddered at the thought and prayed that look would never end up on Conner's face.

"David, say goodbye to your mother for now, she will visit you in a few days to check your mental state." Flanigan said as they were about to exit the room. David was so lost in thought that he had not noticed them walking across the room. With the sound of a click the world went dark again, all that could be seen was the outline of two figures in the doorway as it slowly creaked shut.

David sat there in the dark, the bed now felt cold and no longer welcoming, he was bewildered by what he had just witnessed. So many thoughts were swimming through his mind and he felt a tear trickle down his left cheek. Everything had been so fast and crazy, David hadn't had the time to feel any emotion, let alone remember that emotions were a thing. He tried to stifle a sob and realized he had been holding his breath for a while and his lungs sucked in air without his permission. Then they exhaled the air in a series of hiccups and chokes, he couldn't remember how to breathe.

David was having a panic attack. That feeling when it's thought to be the last step but when stepping forward and there is another one. The feeling of his stomach turning to ice as it turned upside down. The feeling that the floor was ripped out from under him and he has to face a very sudden life altering choice. All of these feelings were hitting him right now. It felt like he had been punched in the gut and couldn't breathe in no matter how hard he had tried to breathe in. Tears started to stream down his face as he clutched his chest in pain due to the burning lack of oxygen.

With the lights being off David couldn't tell that his vision was fading, until he saw dancing colors of greens and blues, these were colors that were only seen when he rubbed his eyes for too long or if he stood up too fast. Then he fell back into the bed in just the same position as he woke up in.

6 GHOST TOWN?

David opened his eyes and he was yet again in a different place. This one was not near as comforting, he was on the ground in the middle of the woods. It was dark and he could hear a faint rustling coming from a bush near to his right. David sat up quickly and grabbed around for a large stick he could use to defend himself. As he picked up the stick nearest to him he heard a small "Mew" that sounded very familiar.

"Melody?" David set the stick down and looked over towards the noise and he could see a pair of glowing yellow eyes near the bottom of the bush. She crawled out and crouching low she inched nearer to him in a cowardly manner. David reached out for her and winced in pain from his arm. He looked down and saw something that horrified him, an eerie, smiling, face was burnt into the flesh on the underside of his forearm. He suddenly remembered his dream and all the eerie smiling. He remembered the figure across the street, how the light showed it's smile that horrified any onlookers. "What is happening?" David whispered as he gathered his knees up with his arms.

He sat there in the middle of the woods with his chin tucked into his knees that he held to his chest, tears started to stream down his cheeks. Melody nuzzled his arm trying to crawl into his lap. He let down his knees; now sitting crisscrossed, she inched her way onto his lap and curled up into a ball. He wiped his tears away with his good arm and slowly stroked Melody with his other arm.

She started to purr at his touch, the sound overpowered everything. David no longer felt fear, he no longer felt sadness, and all that was left was a strength he had not known before. This strength was his will to keep his family and those he cared about safe. He sat there as Melody's Purring enveloped him, that's all he could hear. He could no longer hear the rustling of branches in the wind. He could no longer hear the sound of birds cooing through the night. He could only hear her purring.

David closed his eyes and listened to this sound and let himself be taken by it, he felt more calm and steady. The next thought that entered his mind wasn't one produced by fear, it wasn't produced by anger, or sadness about his mother. This thought was made when the image of Conner, James, and Kaitlyn entered his mind.

I have to keep them safe.

David opened his eyes and looked around to see where he was at. He was in the eastern woods, near where he found the blackberry bush. Picking Melody up off of his lap, he stood up slowly to avoid hurting his arm. Melody nuzzled him and tucked her head into his underarm. The two set off back into the quiet, familiar, dark, and now horrifying town. They reached the bent down wire fencing and climbed over it cautiously, it seemed quiet, even for a small town that barely breathes at night. David looked over to the park with the ballfields, his truck still parked there. He walked quickly through the cold of the night to the truck, he realized he didn't have his keys.

He looked into his truck window to see his keys dangling in the ignition. Melody hopped out of his arms then climbed his shoulder up to the top of the truck and sat on the roof. Infuriated, and full of adrenaline, David grabbed his hand and smashed the window with his elbow. He barely noticed the pain on his arm anymore, he only cared about getting back to his brother. Reaching inside he opened the door then grabbed melody and hopped inside. David turned the keys and the engine roared to life, filling the area with sound.

With Melody asleep in the seat next to him, David sped through the town making his way home. The town was dark, all the street lights were off. He came to the corner where the bookstore was and he turned the corner forgetting to slow down and the force threw melody across the seat hitting the door. She let out a loud *Yowl* and resettled herself, now wide awake. David slowed as he came up to his house and stopped the car right in front of the driveway. He opened the door and ran up to the house, leaving the truck running. The front door was hanging wide open and the frame ripped out of place. "No, this can't happen. Not to Conner." David let out as he stepped inside quaking with anger and fear.

The house was torn to shreds, the coffee table was smashed inwards as if something really heavy had fallen onto it. The couch has been ripped open and stuffing was strewn about on the floor. He yelled out for conner with no answer, it was quiet in the house. In fact it was quiet everywhere, the only noise that could be heard was the truck sitting in the road with Melody waiting inside. David turned to go back outside and on the wall a message was written in black sludge.

Mr. Walker,

I like smiles and this small town is full of them! It seems you have what I want so I would like to play a game! Follow the rules and don't forget… ALWAYS SMILE!

* *:)*

David stared in disbelief, he was terrified and dumbfounded. He was so angry and filled with so much emotion that the next words said, he yelled at the top of his lungs. "WHAT GAME?!"

He punched the wall and screamed with tears running down his cheeks. A thud came from his bedroom and startled him. He wiped the tears from his eyes and slowly headed towards his bedroom to see what made the sound. As he approached the bedroom, he noticed the door was closed but he could hear a rustling on the other side. David reached for the door handle hesitantly, then with a creaking sound, the door opened. His eyes widened with relief and surprise by what he saw. Though the relief was small, he was no longer alone with just Melody.

"James?" David said with urgent surprise.

7 PUZZLES AND GAMES

James was laying on the bed with his hands bound behind his back and legs tied so he couldn't move. His restraints weren't rope or anything that David has seen before, they were made of a black fleshy rope. He had the same stuff covering his mouth, though it was hardened and worked sort of like duct-tape.

"What happened to you?" David asked as he walked over to James who was struggling to get free. "I'm gonna try to get you out." David went to his bedside table and opened it to look for his knife. When he looked inside he didn't find his knife, but instead found a piece of paper with a black rock next to it. He pulled out the paper and started to read it out loud to James.

Mr. Walker,

I absolutely adore games! They make me smile! This one shall be fun, you must play along or Mr. Haul will not make it to tomorrow. It is simple enough, you must get the shiphile off of your partner, that is if you want him to come along with you on this journey of insanity that you call life. This is your first encounter with my puzzles so I shall be generous. I have given you a give you a gift and a hint!

- *:)*

"What is a shiphile?" David asked as he finished reading the paper and looked at James who was now sitting up a bit, waiting to be freed. David flipped the paper over to find the clue written on the back, a series of words.

SPOURMO

TREEALOP

ONAMA

NOVALY

ETHOSIEN

SWOQUIX

MOLDEF

IGROD

LOPLAB

EPSORE

BESLORE

LUEZOID

OLUEWO

OCIRASSI

DIDIZA

SOHAAN

HESTUR

IMOE

PLAKILE

HESTYBUS

IBRID

LINTRUE

EILIU

David looked up from the paper after reading these strange words to James, he was confused and could barely pronounce half of them. He looked at James to see if he knew what they meant. James was staring off into the distance puzzled and thinking as hard as he could. David then went back to the drawer and picked up the black rock.

"Ouch" David yelped as he slit the tip of his finger open on the side of the rock. "It's sharp on this side... Maybe I can use it to cut that stuff off of you!" James looked up at David in hopes that he was right. Next, James shuffled on the bed so that his back was facing David, holding his arms out as much as he could, so they may be freed. David took the rock and held it up to the black gunk attempting to cut it away. He pushed harder at the gunk but it wouldn't even bend the stuff.

David's hand slipped and nicked James's wrist, to which James winced in pain and grunted. His wrist started to bleed out a small amount and a drop of his blood landed on the fleshy restraints. The black gunk responded to the blood with sizzling and constricting his wrists even more. James tightened his muscles in pain and turned red in the face, he felt like his hands were going to be ripped off.

"James! I'm sorry, I don't know what to do." David said in frustration. He became enraged and threw the stone at the wall as hard as he could. The restraints loosened up back to their original state and James let out a sigh of relief. David sank to his knees, wanting to give up, wanting it to end. After James caught his breath he looked over to where the paper was laying on the bedside table. He noticed the layout of the Words on the back and grunted at David to look at it again.

"What? I already read it. It's just a bunch of gobbledygook…" David said in reply. To this James shook his head and grunted again. David decided to give in and look at the paper once more. "Which side did you see something, the back?" David asked. James shook his head to agree with David. He picked up the paper again and looked at the back, this time studying any patterns he could find. David's eyes suddenly opened wide and looked at James. "Four words! There are four words!" David shouted. David quickly went to his dresser and grabbed a pen off the top and quickly scribbled down four words. *STONE, SMILE, BLOOD, SHIPHILE.*

"Well, we have four words but what do they mean. The first one is stone, that must be the stone that was in the drawer." David announced as he went to pick up the rock off the floor. "The next word is smile? So we have a sharp rock and the third word is blood. I had a dream the other day where I cut a smile into Conner's mouth maybe it's something like that?" David thought hard and James looked confused and scared at this thought. David thought about what the word smile could mean and he remembered his arm. Looking at his arm he noticed that it no longer hurt it just looked like scar tissue. "What i'm about to do is to save you, you aren't allowed to get mad at me, okay?" David sounded grim, James only looked confused and concerned.

David took the stone in his left hand and gripped it tightly. He closed his eyes and started to tear into his arm with the sharp end of the stone. Blood trickled out of the scarred smiley face and dripped to the floor. James winced and closed his eyes, The sight was awful to witness. David dropped the rock and cupped his hand under his wrist to catch the blood. He walked over to James holding his own blood in his hands.

"The shiphile, it's your restraints, we have to smear the blood, cut out from the smile on my arm with the stone, onto the shiphile." David said solemnly as he started to smear the blood onto the shiphile on James's feet. James looked at his feet and watched in awe as it started to bubble and loosen. It looked as if it were shrinking away and was rotting quickly. The shiphile shriveled into nothing and James could move his legs freely at last. David quickly moved from the feet up to the wrists and smeared more blood onto that set of shiphile, it too melted away in a similar manner.

James stood up off of the bed and faced david, who was holding his wrist which was dripping blood. David was looking dazed as he was losing blood. So James pulled him in for a hug and held him. Their bodies so close that they could become one. David let his weight be held by James and he regained some strength when he remembered that there was only one part left, the mouth. David looked up at James, he became lost in his swimming blue eyes, forgetting what he had to do next. James closed his eyes and David did as well, they pressed their foreheads together and let the world pause for a moment. David then took his hand, now covered in blood, and brought it up to James's cheek. The blood forced the shiphile to rot quickly away from his hand.

When they opened their eyes, they were staring into one another's and sat there in the silence, staring. David was the one to break the silence, "I'm sorry…" he said in a small voice. To this James only had one reply, it wasn't words, but it was worth more than words could ever mean. James tilted his head and leaned in, kissing David. Instantly, David wrapped his arms around him, soaking his shirt in blood, he no longer felt the burning sensation in his wrist or the cold from the blood loss. They kissed in silence, allowing the world to melt away, even if it was only for a moment.

They broke away and David looked at James in shock but he was happy, happy that James was okay. David couldn't resist and he pulled James in and hugged him tightly, not wanting to let go in fear of losing him. Suddenly a hissing sound could be heard over the sound of the running truck outside.

"Melody!" David shouted and broke away from James and ran towards the door to see what was happening.

"David wait!" James called after him and began to chase David out the door.

8 RECUPERATION

David ran through the living room, passing the writing on the wall not noticing that it had changed. He had ran past it and out the door in a whirlwind of adrenaline and fury. "Don't touch my cat!" David shouted through tears as he was tired of everything and delirious from blood loss. James only followed him as far as the living room and he noticed the writing on the wall. It read something completely different and struck James on a different chord, he became infuriated by what he read.

Mr. Walker,

Well done, you saved him! You fairies always surprise me, I never would've thought that a halfwit faggot could figure out something that intelligent. I can't wait for you to see what else I have in store for you and your boy toy! Maybe together YOU WILL SMILE MORE!

- *:)*

David walked back in with his head hanging because he had not found Melody, he looked up when he noticed James holding a leg from the coffee table in his hand. James was fuming, he lifted the leg of the table and smashed it against the wall. David flinched at the loud crash that put a hole right in the center of the message, then David read it and realized why he was so enraged. He walked up to James and softly put his hand on the leg to stop him from doing any more damage.

James turned around and solemnly looked at David, "I'm sorry…" he said in a voice that was almost whispering.

"For what?" David responded "This isn't your fault, you didn't do anything wrong." He pulled James away from the wall, hugging him tightly. "This isn't anyone's fault."

"We will get through this okay, we'll make it out and I'll be able to take you to that burger place." James said as David wiped away a few tears that had escaped and he let out a small laugh.

"Okay, we'll do that as soon as this is over." He said as he pulled James in for another hug before they headed out to the truck.

The truck was driving through the empty town, there were no sounds or light. The only sound that could be heard was the trucks groaning as it drove down the deserted roads. "Where is everyone?" David asked feeling queasy from the emptiness.

"I don't know, all I remember is going to bed and then waking up in this cave like bush. I tried to get out to figure out where I was but I couldn't move. It felt like I was trapped in a dream that I couldn't wake up from." James explained.

"How did you get to my house? Bound with that Shiphile stuff?"

"Well, I sat there in the bush/cave thing for what felt like a day. I fell asleep after a while and then I woke up because I heard something coming in through a hole that was close to the ground."

David hit the brakes as he came to an intersection in the west part of town. "Wait, was it over in the eastern woods? Just past the bent down fence?" He questioned while staring into a memory of the blackberry bush.

"I have no idea, why?" James looked a little concerned.

"The other day I was looking for Melody when I found this blackberry bush. I crawled inside of it to see if she had gone in there. My phone light wouldn't turn on so I looked around in the dark. The only thing in there other than me was…"

"Was what? I never saw anything other than whatever crawled through there... almost touched me then left, I couldn't see it very well though."

"James, what if that thing was me, and what I saw sitting on the other side of the room was you?"

"It couldn't have been, It spoke a strange language, not any I have ever heard before."

"James, we need to go back to that bush… it might tell us some more about what's been happening here."

David cranked the steering wheel and made a U-turn, the truck was suddenly headed east. The two sat in silence for a while, frightened by the events of that day. The quiet went on for ten minutes until David broke the silence again.

"What do you think those words were?" He asked remembering the strange words written on the back of the paper.

"They were pseudowords, words that sound like they are real words but have no meaning other than confusion." James replied with surprising readiness.

"Well what was that shiphile stuff and why did it react to my blood that way?" David asked tightening some makeshift bandages he put on before leaving the house.

"I have no idea, I woke up in the bed after passing out in the blackberry bush. That stuff was covering me and the more I struggle, the tighter it got." James replied quietly.

The truck slowed as they came near to the entrance of the park, there was a figure standing in a cone of light coming from the only working streetlamp. David hit the brakes, stopping the vehicle, the two sat gaping at the figure. The figure wasn't moving and they didn't know how to respond, up until this point they were the only two in town.

"Who is that?" David stuttered, not taking his eyes off of the figure. James reached into the back seat to look for a blunt object in case they needed to fight. "Are we planning on going up there?" David asked looking concerned.

"How else are we gonna figure out what's happening? By sitting in the truck for the rest of the night?" James said sarcastically. James reached for the handle and opened the truck door.

"Wait, I'm coming with you." David said as he put the truck in park. David reached under his seat and grabbed a machete that he keeps in his truck, in case it breaks down in the middle of nowhere and he needs it. David opened his door and the two took off towards the figure on the other side of the park. They crossed the small bridge, that separated the park from the gravel parking lot, and kept an eye on the figure as they slowly made their way forward.

The figure let out a small voice that sounded rattled and exhausted.

"Help…. Me…" It cried out. David and James quickly raced to the figure only to realize it was a person stuck to a wooden post with spikes driven through different parts of their body. It was Kaitlyn, she was held up to the post like a scarecrow and she looked torn and beaten.

"Kaitlyn!" James yelled as David dropped to his knees, holding his stomach. David was stunned by the sight, he felt nauseous and appalled.

"Help…. Me…" She cried out again, not noticing James and David. Her eyes were glazed over with a white film and she was no longer attached to reality. James tried to console her as he frantically tried to find ways to get her down.

"Help…. Me…" She called out as blood leaked from different spikes. David regained his ability to stand and hustled over to help James.

"Help…. Me…" She whispered as they gave up, realizing that if they removed a single spike, she would bleed out and die.

"Help…. Me…" She let out one last call for help before her head dropped and any motion in her ceased to exist. Kaitlyn was dead, she was strung up and humiliated, there was nothing that they could do to save her. David again sank to his knees and started to sob, James only stared in disbelief. They felt the heaviness of the situation, it was no longer puzzles and games, this was real. David's sobs turned to hiccups and his breaths became short and heavy. His panic attack returned, the dancing lights did as well, and he fell backwards. The last thing he saw before the world went dark was Kaitlyn's Dazed eyes staring and empty.

9 REALITY?

When David started to come to again, he was in a bed. The
bed was small and familiar, he had been here before. He opened
his eyes to complete darkness and sat up. David's stomach dropped
as he realized it was the Blue Hearth Clinic. Slowly standing up,
David hoped to find the lights by walking towards the other side of
the room. He felt like he had walked far and he couldn't see
anything. There was no way of telling how far he had left before he
made it. David stretched his arms out in front of him to feel for the
wall and with a few more steps, he made it to the other side.

David felt around for a few moments before finding the lights
and then a click was heard. The room lit up shortly after and that
was followed by a small humming sound that was coming from the
overhead lights. David let his eyes adjust then he looked around
the room. When he looked, all he could see was a normal room; it
had a bed, a dresser, and a bedside table with a lamp on it. Taking
a few steps forward he noticed something on the bedside table, it
was an empty pill bottle laying on its side.

David walked closer and picked up the pill bottle reading it's
label. He squirmed a bit when he read it to himself.

David A Walker

Take three pills by mouth daily : One pill for every meal : Treats severe schizophrenia and bipolar disorders : Side effects include Vomiting, Diarrhea, Blackouts, Hallucinogenic Episodes, and Vertigo

David couldn't believe what he had read, had he been in a dream this whole time? He decided to check out more of the clinic, only to walk to the door and discover it was locked. He went and sat on the bed thinking about different ways to get out of the room without making himself known. As he sat, he began sweeping his hands across the sheets because of how soft they were, this gave him a thought. David excitedly looked up to find a window, though there were no windows for him to break by wrapping his hands with sheets.

He stood up when he noticed a vent on the other side of the room next to the dresser. Walking over to it, he suddenly became very cold. It felt like he was crossing the room in sub freezing temperatures. By the time he had made it halfway across the room his legs started to freeze up and he could barely move forward. David was determined to make it to the vent, something was there, he knew there had to be something.

After taking a few more steps, he noticed something on the other side of the vent, it looked like a pair of eyes, just barely glowing in the dark. David held his arms, hugging himself to keep warm, yet he kept moving forward. His vision started to blur and he had to squint to see anything straight. The cold became unbearable and he sank to his knees, shivering obstreperously. He looked up one more time, staring hard at the vent with the eyes, and out of his mouth came words that he couldn't keep from saying.

"What is real?" he let out in almost a whisper.

David then laid down on the floor and curled up to keep warm. The shivering and the cold overtook him. Suddenly all of his muscles relaxed and his eyes closed, he felt warm. The darkness felt inviting and he gave in, walking freely into a slumber.

Back on the bed, David laid in the darkness for what felt like hours. He laid perfectly still because no matter what he tried, he couldn't move. Suddenly the door opened and the lights flicked on. Dr. Flanigan could be heard at the door "Mr. Walker, it's time for meds and breakfast." David was able to move as soon as those words left Dr. Flanigan's mouth. As David sat up, Flanigan left the room leaving him to get dressed and ready for the day.

David stretched, happy he was finally able to move. He looked over to the dresser and he noticed something that wasn't there the night before. There was a calendar pinned to the wall just above it. He walked over to inspect it further. It had a picture of puppy snuggled up with a kitten in front of a window with snow outside of it. The month was December, David was confused by the month. "It's August, winter is nowhere close." He muttered as he pulled it off the wall.

On the calendar there were several days crossed out. This meant that today was the seventeenth, which according to the calendar was movie night. Strangely that was written in David's handwriting, as was a note that David spotted on the dresser. Sitting next to the note was a newly filled pill bottle and a glass of water. He picked up the note and read it to himself.

Day 106

- _Take pills_ **DO NOT TAKE!!!**
- _Get dressed: Clothes in top drawer_
- _Use restroom_ **DON'T TRUST THE MIRROR**
- _Report for morning roll call_ **DO NOT MISS**
- _Game room_ **FIND STRANGER!!!**
- _Lunch and Meds_ **STILL DON'T TAKE!!!**
- _MOVIE NIGHT!_
- _Dinner and Meds_ **YOU KNOW THE DRILL!**
- _Bed_
- **DO NOT SLEEP!!!**
- **ESCAPE!**
- **FIND CONNER!**

David set the note down and scratched his head. "Did I write this?" He said aloud as he opened the top drawer. Inside was a set of clothes just as the note had said. David was happy to get out of his clothes… that were now clean? He looked down and noticed he was wearing different clothes than he remembered. These clothes were pajamas, not normal pajamas, more like hospital ones. He undressed and grabbed the clothes out of the drawer. There was some underwear, a white t-shirt, and a greenish outfit that is usually seen on nurses and doctors. David felt light in these clothes, he felt like he could move more freely.

He looked at the pills and, remembering the note, decided not to take one. Instead he took one out of the bottle and tossed it into the vent, then he drank the water, this way it would look like he had taken his pill. Next he stuffed the note into his pocket in case it was needed for later. Cautiously he reached for the door, up until this moment he had not seen any other parts of the clinic. The knob turned and the door clicked open with ease. Outside of the door was a long hall stretching to his left and right. Hanging on the wall right in front of his door was a sign that had two arrows; the one to the left had 200-300 written above it, and the one to the right had the words Dining Hall written above it.

David decided to go to the right, towards the dining hall. As he walked further down the hall he could hear voices coming from a room on his left. He came across another sign, next to a door with a window, this one had named the room as Game Room. Looking through the window he saw many people milling about. Some were sitting at tables playing games like chess and checkers, others were sitting on sofas watching a television. As David looked closer at the people who were in the room he noticed a familiar face sitting next to the window. The town sheriff, Scott Reynolds, was sitting in a wheelchair staring blankly out to a courtyard.

Opening the door, David quickly made his way over to where Scott was at. Next to him was a small table with checkers on it, an empty chair sitting opposite of him. David pulled the chair out and sat down gaping at the sheriff, he looked dead inside.

"Scott?" David whispered, he was stunned by the sheriff's presence in a place like this. Suddenly his dead eyes winked to life, there was a glimmer in his green eyes that just seconds ago seemed grey.

"Ah David, would you like to play a round of checkers? I've been waiting to verse someone all morning." Scott said as he turned to face David and smiling. David was stunned and didn't know how to respond. Suddenly the sheriff's face became grim and serious. "You look like you have woken from a bad dream. If you play me at checkers we can talk about this *dream*." Scott said quietly as if telling a secret. He had put so much emphasis on the word 'dream' that David could only wonder if he knew what was happening.

"Oh, yeah… I guess i'll play." David said as Scott started to set up the checkerboard,

"Red or Black?" Scott announced as he gathered the pieces.

"Your choice"

"Ah, but don't you see? That's not how this game works. I make the rules and you follow them. If you want to beat me at my own game then you must first learn how to play." Scott spoke these words as if he weren't talking about checkers at all. David looked up from the board and the two met eyes. The sheriff winked. "Now listen closely because this game is really complicated, you will be red.

10 THE CLINIC

"Okay?" David said starting to realize that there was something behind this game of checkers that might help him out later. Scott slid over five red pieces, one of the pieces was faded and had a yellow star on the face of it. As David studied the board and the pieces; he realized that they were strange. It seemed like an old set but they also looked brand new, like it had never been opened.

"So the board has two sides right? Side R for regular..." Scott said as he flipped the board over. On this side the board was green and white instead of the normal black and red. "...and side I for irregular." He flipped the board back to the black and red side.

"What's the difference between the two sides?" Davis asked.

"Well, side R is played by the normal rules and everything is how you see it. Side I is not so easy, pieces come back and multiply." Scott looked a bit distant when he was talking about side I. Next he started setting his pieces down on the board. There were six black pieces and one was faded with a silver-green star on its face.

"How is that fair? You getting six pieces while I have five." David said a bit frustrated. When David said this, Scott became irritated and pulled out two more black pieces and set them out.

"It's fair because you need to learn that this isn't fair. Fairness isn't how you win this game, it's how you lose." Scott said as David grudgingly nodded and set out his pieces. "The one with the star is your leader, if you lose him then the game is over and the opposing team wins. Any black piece can kill the red star but only the red star can beat the black star."

"So how am I supposed to safely get my star to take yours?" David questioned starting to regret playing.

"Side I will be where you want to be but to get there you must sacrifice a piece." When Scott made this comment he made a wink. This wink hinted at a different way to get to Side I. "Oh and one more rule before we start, Black gets two turns and Red only gets one."

"But that makes it impossible to win!" David was now sitting with his arms crossed and refused to play.

"If you refuse to play that is your choice but doing so will make it easy for Black to win. Not only will Black win but he will enjoy killing of every one of your pieces before he gets to you." Scott announced as he took his star and knocked the Red pieces off of the board one by one leaving only the star piece. Then as he looked at David he grabbed the star piece and broke it in half.

David looked at him concerned, the way Scott described this last part felt too real to be a game. Scott dropped the pieces and his eyes went blank again he stared right through David. A small giggle could be heard, it was coming from Scott, his laugh grew louder and louder until David noticed people coming to take him away. He quickly got up and left the room so he didn't get caught. As David traveled a bit further down the hall he felt anxious and sick to his stomach, was that game more than just a game?

He walked past a restroom realizing he hadn't gone the the bathroom for a long time. This made him have to go really badly, so he opened the door and headed inside. After using the urinal to relieve himself he walked to the sinks to wash his hands. Out of the corner of his eye he saw something in the mirror.

When he looked up he was chilled by the sight of his reflection. He was smiling… The reflection was actually smiling. David started to feel his face to see if it was him or the reflection that was the one smiling, only to find out that the reflection didn't feel its face. His heart started to race and he had regrets about not taking the medicine, he might be seeing things. He left the bathroom frightened about what might happen if he had stayed. After calming himself he walked a little further down the hall and found the dining hall.

When pushing the doors open, he noticed that he interrupted roll call. This was because it was completely silent in the room, even with the 50 people that were now staring at him. The silence made the sound of the door amplify and he felt as if he had slammed it.

"David Walker," a man announced "glad to see you could finally join us." The man did not sound amused about his entrance.

"Sorry, I uh… had to use the restroom…" David responded with a shiver remembering the reflection.

The man then continued calling out names and repeating them until you could hear an unenthusiastic "Here" and David made his way to a table in the back.

"Breakfast will now be served, please make an orderly line and be patient." The man said in a way that showed he would rather be watching grass grow than to be here. All the patients obediently began to form a line and started filing through to get their breakfast. David was stuck in between a very scrawny woman and a very tall, gruff man. As the line moved they all picked up trays and proceeded to have different foods plopped onto them. The food was all different shades of browns, greens, and greys, although they all had the same texture, gloopy and wet.

The woman in front of David turned to him and whispered "Can I have your milk?" He wasn't in the mood for a meal so he nodded his head and she whispered again "Wait until we get to the table to give it to me." She looked very timid and it seemed like sharing food was evidently not allowed. So he waited until they made it through the line and she pulled him along to the back corner to a table.

The gruff looking man followed silently and set his tray across from David's. He sat down and stared right into David's eyes. "I don't trust him Jane, he seems like he knows something." The man said in a low, disapproving tone.

"Listen he can help, I've been watching him for a week now." Jane replied, she sounded like she was trying really hard to persuade him. They talked about David as if he wasn't there until he cleared his throat reminding them *who* they were talking about.

"Oh hi! I'm Jane" She said suddenly enthusiastic and bright. "and this is Vinny! he may seem scary but he is actually really nice." Vinny only grunted and nodded his head, refusing to talk to David. "So I'm guessing you wanna know what we were talking about huh?"

"Well just a tad. Considering you were talking about me." David said sarcastically. He was starting to get annoyed with these two but he was also relieved to have a distraction from all that's happening.

"Well…" she said quietly while eyeing around the room. "Vinny, some others, and I are planning an escape."

"An escape? Why do you need to escape? Also why do you need me, I wouldn't be of much use." David asked looking concerned.

"See Jane? I told you he couldn't." Vinny finally piped up "He could ruin it for all of us." He leaned back and crossed his arms.

"Look, I've been watching you for a week, I've learned certain things about you." Jane said ignoring Vinny.

"What have you learned, I have yet to figure certain things out myself." David said, talking more to himself than the others.

"Well for starters you forget everything from the previous day as soon as you wake up. Also you have an ability to get around this place without getting caught, which is weird because guards are everywhere. So that could help us a lot." She continued rambling off different things as David zoned out thinking about the first comment she said.

"What do you mean I forget everything?" David questioned, cutting her off.

"Well you go through your day learning everything about this place and a bunch of its secrets, then before I get the chance to talk to you, we go to bed and the next morning you forget everything except for who you are and some story about some smiling dude." She said this as if it were normal and nothing about it was weird or unusual. Before David could reply a bell rang and people started making to the doors, breakfast was over. "Okay, meet us in the game room by the TV. Don't tell anyone." Then they got up and left, as if the conversation didn't even happen.

David walked out of the lunchroom and followed the crowd down the hall a bit before hearing a buzzing sound coming from a door leading to a separate hallway. He peeked through the windows and didn't see anything of importance. Nobody else seemed to be phased by the sound but David's curiosity grew, this place just seemed so strange. He looked around and waited for the last few people to walk by then he quietly opened the door to the second hallway. Slipping through into the new hallway, he heard the door click shut and the drilling was silenced. A light overhead flickered and David instantly felt a sense of anxiety, he wasn't supposed to be in this area. The lights in this hall were a yellow color compared to the blue of the other lights in the building.

David could hear footsteps from around a corner so he quickly jumped behind the door to his left. He left the door slightly creaked open so he could hear if he needed. The footsteps drew nearer and became louder so David looked through the crack to see if he could tell who was there. Though he could hear the footsteps walk right past the door, he saw nothing. There was no man to match the sound of the walking. David stared at the floor where the footsteps were and waited anxiously, not knowing why there wasn't a person there.

Suddenly David felt a tug on his shirt from behind and he nearly had a heart attack. He turned around to see a young boy, who looked to be about five or six years old. He was wearing pinstripe pajamas and holding a torn stuffed animal.

"Can you hear them too?" The boy said in a whisper as he brought the stuffed animal close to his chest holding it tight. The boy looked scared and David was concerned for him.

"What?" David hadn't realized he had been asked a question. "Oh, the footsteps?"

"Mhm, they come every two hours but I'm the only one who hears them." The boy said calmly, though he looked young he spoke with a mature dialect. David looked back out the door to see if there was anyone there. "I'm Quincy, everyone calls me Q though. What are you doing in my room mister?"

"I don't think I'm supposed to be in this hall so I hid in here when I heard the footsteps. Did you say you're the only one who can hear them?" David asked starting to accept the random events that make no sense.

"Mhm, and sometimes they also open my door." Q replied as if this were normal. "I don't talk about them any more because they will give me another fit again and I don't like having fits." David wondered what he meant by a 'fit', maybe he had seizures or something. The footsteps had finally ceased and David was ready to get back to where he was supposed to be.

"Well I have to go before they notice me." David said as he started opening the door. "It was nice meeting you Q, I'll come back and we can talk again."

"David?" Q's voice sounded more sad than previous and he sounded as if he were about to break into tears.

"Yeah?"

"I want to see my mommy again, will you take me?" Q asked this then yawned and walked back to his bed not waiting for an answer.

"Yes" David answered in a whisper feeling like he needed to help this child in any way possible.

As David closed the door and started heading towards the hall, he had heard voices coming from the bathrooms to his left, he listened closely. The voices were not doctors or patients, it sounded like James, Connor, and even Kaitlyn. He headed straight for the door, the sound of Kaitlyn's voice was mesmerizing, she was dead.

He opened the bathroom doors and the voices stopped but he could see three mirrors, each had a figure standing in them. None were his own reflection, but instead it was the three people he had missed most: Conner, James, and Kaitlyn. They were staring blankly to the opposite side of the wall, David stared in disbelief until they started to shift. Their forms melted away and left in their place were three new figures, Jane, Vinny, and Q. He stared in disbelief and felt unable to move. The three figures represented the three people he missed? which one's were real?

Suddenly they were no longer facing the wall, they were now facing him. Their eyes held anger. David could feel their eyes piercing right through him, this anger was infectious. He could feel himself becoming enraged. He was lost in a loop between two worlds in which he had no idea which one was real. Without thinking he raised his fist and smashed the mirror in the middle. His hand flew straight through the mirror. It shattered, but behind it was a hole. Large enough to crawl through, it was more of a tunnel than a hole. The figures in the other two mirrors silently pointed towards the entrance, exhorting him to go in.

Before David could decide to leave the bathroom, something crawled out of the tunnel, it was a small spider. It crawled down the wall and onto the floor. David's gaze followed the spider as it crawled under and through his legs. He turned around to see the spider crawl a bit further and then it stopped, suddenly a foot smashed down onto the spider, pouring its guts out in a splatter. David almost screamed but had no time before a forceful hand shoved him into the tunnel. He fell backwards and hit his head on a sharp rock and his vision started to fade, all that he could see was the town sheriff, Scott Reynolds, standing at the entrance. With a smile that reached from ear to ear.

11 TUNNELING SECRETS

As David's vision finally came back into focus he looked around to see what had happened. Looking back where he came from, he noticed the hole in the mirror had closed behind him. He tried to stand but the tunnel was too shallow and he had to crawl to move. As he felt around in the now darkened tunnel he found that it lead down further. He traveled along the tunnel on his hands and knees for what felt like half an hour before he needed a break. He sat with his back against the wall and his knees up against his chest.

"Ouch" David yelped as he rubbed his hands together. There was a faint light in the tunnel now so he could see his hands. They were bleeding. He had been crawling in the tunnel for so long that he wore the skin away at his palms and most likely his knees as well. Suddenly the floor gave way and David was falling. He grasped at his surroundings trying to grab onto the sides of the tunnel but the fall was too sudden.

He was again plunged into darkness, this time falling. The fall felt as if it was taking too long, how high had he been. He no longer felt the adrenaline of the drop, in fact it felt as if he were floating instead of falling. David reached his arms out to see if he could touch anything but felt no walls. The rush of wind felt nice on his skin from being in the cramped tunnel for so long. Then as David was about to scream out for something to happen a light started to shine, it was coming from his left. It was small and dim, just barely visible. It must have been falling with him because it was staying in the same spot.

As the little light grew brighter David could see a bit more of his surroundings. He looked at the walls and they were just out of reach, he was in a cylindrically shaped room. Then he noticed something strange, the walls weren't speeding past him as if he were falling. He was floating, the wind was pushing him up in the air. His heart began to race as he looked downwards. He saw water, the bottom was filled with black water. He couldn't see underneath of the water and this made his stomach queasy, as he was floating above it. Just before he looked back up he noticed a ripple of movement in the water. Then he saw something big move the still water. A large shadow could be seen swimming upwards towards the surface but not breaking it and then back down.

Then David heard a noise, it sounded like a click and a chittering sound. He looked up towards the noise to see something he had wished to not see. Looking at the source of light he saw that it was being generated by a giant spider-like creature. It had several limbs that were long and clasped onto the wall, one limb was rubbing the creature's head. Which couldn't be seen because the light was coming from what seemed to be its eyes. The only feature that could be made out was the mandibles that were large and looked very sharp. The light was trained on David and his heart almost stopped at the thought of this thing jumping towards him.

Suddenly as the creature was about to leap into the air, claiming its next meal, the airflow cut out. David started falling and he dipped straight into the waters. The water was ice and David could barely breathe. He swam back to the surface and took a huge gasp of air, he could hear a screeching sound filled with clicks and chatters then he watched as the creature crawled into a hole in the wall. David swam towards the edge as the light fizzled away. He felt along the wall for some form of exit. He wanted out of the water as soon as he could. Then the water started to feel different, it was abnormally still. David felt choked by the quiet and calm, he quickly followed the wall using his hands as guidance in the dark. Then he felt it, the water began to ripple. He felt something swimming from the other side of the room, it felt huge. The water around him began to rise and his heart began to race. Then just as the thing started towards him, a rope was thrown down.

David quickly grabbed the rope and was suddenly being pulled upwards. A bright light pointed down at him from the source of the rope and blinded David. He quickly shut his eyes from the pain of the light and looked down. When he opened his eyes he saw the waters and saw the shadow of the giant swimming downwards, out of the light.

"Hey! David, is that you?" a voice shouted. David shielded his eyes against the light to see who had helped him. Jane and Vinny! David had been saved by his two new friends.

"Jane? Vinny? How did you find me?" David replied as they pulled him up onto the ledge. As he grabbed at a rock and tried to gain his footing, Vinny gave him a steadying hand.

"We saw that you disappeared and thought you decided to escape without us." Vinny said broodingly.

"Vinny wanted to leave you behind, but I wouldn't allow it!" chimed Jane. Even in the worst situation, she seemed to always be bright and cheery. "We found a tunnel in the ventilation system and followed it until we dropped into this cave. Then we heard this screeching sound and splashing, so we came to investigate. that's where we found you!"

"We're glad you're alive…" Vinny mumbled looking at the ground, avoiding eye contact.

"Anyways, what happened with you?" Jane announced as they all sat against walls to catch up on what's happening. "You just kinda disappeared."

"I was looking at some mirrors and then I kinda broke one. But there was a tunnel behind it and before I could stop it, someone surprised me and shoved me inside." David explained quickly. Vinny looked concerned for David, but when they met eyes Vinny quickly looked away and shuffled in his spot. "Hey Vin-" David was cut off when the screeching sound from that creature came back. It must have heard them talking.

They took off, running down the tunnel being chased by this creature, its long arms just barely missing them. With The light from Vinny's flashlight, more features could be seen. It had one eye that was large and yellow, it looked like as if it were made of glass. On top of its head was a bare spot that look as if it had been rubbed raw for years. Its mandibles seemed ten times more menacing than they had before, with several spikes jutting out from them.

Suddenly the creature lifted back one of its arms and started rubbing at the bare spot, it's eye started to glow. At first it was a small light but as they ran, the light grew stronger, almost blinding them. Jane's foot got caught on a rock and she face planted into the side of the tunnel, knocking some of the dirt loose. The creature didn't hesitate, it quickly shot out a limb to grab her and she was caught by the same foot that tripped her. Vinny stopped and turned to face the creature, he had the hatred of the gods in his eyes. He started towards the monster as it pulled the screaming girl towards it's mandibles. This surprised the creature and it scuttled into the darkness, dragging Jane along with it.

Vinny screamed and threw a large rock towards the darkness the creature had disappeared in. Then he sank to his knees in disbelief as Jane's screams slowly faded away. David walked up to Vinny and laid his hand of the gruff man's shoulder. He didn't say anything because he didn't know what to say. David was already numb from pain, especially after witnessing Kaitlyn's death.

"I'm going…" Vinny said in almost a whisper. David just nodded his head, there was no use in arguing as Vinny was delirious with anger. Vinny stood up and pointed the flashlight towards the darkness that creature fled into. Then without hesitation he marched forward into this perilous task. David watched as Vinny entered the hole in the side of the tunnel that the creature had left in, then with a big huff, he followed.

After a minute or two David finally caught up to Vinny, breathing heavily from the pace he had to walk. It was silent and neither spoke. They just trudged forward following the twisting tunnel, hoping to find the creature's hideout, hoping it wasn't too late.

12 WORLDS COLLIDE

Q was sitting in his bed alone when the footsteps started to walk by his room again. He winced when the door was opened, wishing that they would just go away. He closed his eyes and squeezed his torn owl as hard as he could. The door suddenly slammed shut and the footsteps walked nearer. Q's breaths became short and heavy as they got closer to his bed. His head felt as if it were vibrating and the room suddenly started vibrating too. Q started to scream as it started to hurt his head. Then a voice could be heard "Quincy! Calm down!" the voice yelled at above all the noise. Q gasped and opened his eyes to see Dr. Flanagin leaning against the wall holding his head, his clipboard on the ground and papers strewn about.

Q stared in disbelief at what he did, did he really do that? Dr. Flanagin picked up his clipboard and papers then took a step towards Q. In response Q winced, Flanagin was mad. Whenever he got mad, he would do bad things. The doctor stepped closer to Q, his face red with anger.

"How dare you do that? Do you need another lesson Quincy?" He growled, his voice low and irate.

"Please... I... I didn't mean to..." Q said as his voices broke into tears. He cowered in his bed holding his owl up to his face, soaking it in fearful tears. Dr. Flanagin raised his fist, in it was the clipboard. Q couldn't bring his arms up in time to block the blow. The clipboard struck him right next to his eye, splitting the skin open. Yelping in pain he held his arms up to his face to try and hide from Flanagin. The doctor just laughed at the sight of the crying boy and turned to leave.

As he reached for the door, Q stopped crying; suddenly fearless, he felt as if he could do anything. Flanagin opened the door and it was suddenly slammed shut by Q. He had merely looked at the door and he was able to forcefully close it. Dr. Flanagin had jumped nearly 3 feet away from the door and turned to look back. Doing so caused him to drop his clipboard again, he had made direct eye contact with the boy. Q stared him down and suddenly the man was starting to rise up into the air. He tried to scream but his voice was cut off as Q tilted his head to the side. Q's eyes were blank yet they were filled with emotion, he wouldn't even blink. The light in the room had started to buzz very loudly and then it started to flicker. Q's power was so immense that it felt as if the pressure in the room was strangling Flanigan. Suddenly the doctor's face was turning red, he really couldn't breathe. He struggled trying to bring his hands to his throat, his limbs were held outwards by an unseen force.

Q whispered something, it was silent yet filled with hatred and power.

"No more."

With the sound of his voice, the floating man had burst into bits. His blood and flesh splattered every part of the room, it was sudden and the only part that it missed was Quincy. The pressure in the room had dissipated just as suddenly as Dr. Flanagin had popped. There was no longer pressure but the aura around Quincy was dark and flowing. He stood at the edge of the bed, his bare feet touching down into a puddle of flesh where he picked up his blood-soaked stuffed owl. The patter of his feet in the gore echoed as he walked towards the door.

When Q got to the door, he didn't even twitch and it flew off of its hinges into the hall. The silence that ensued after was stagnant, as if his aura sucked the sound out of the air. He held his owl in his left hand as he walked down the hall, leaving footprints of Dr. Flanigan's blood trailing behind him. The muffled sound of footsteps could be heard coming from down the hall and around a corner. Q didn't react, as if he couldn't hear them, he just walked forward. Two workers turned the corner, they were talking to each other but their voices weren't audible. As they looked up, noticing Q walking and leaving a bloody trail, they tried to dart at him. As soon as they took a step forward a force had blown them to opposite sides of the hallway. Q had stopped walking for a split second waiting for the hall to be clear. One worker had been thrown into a wall, knocking him breathless, he was held up to the wall unable to move.

What he had to witness while pinned to the wall was something no man should see. The other worker was forcefully lifted but not quickly. His limbs were held out, just as Dr. Flanagan's. He was being held in place while the piping on the wall behind him suddenly bent outwards towards the man's back. When the piping stopped bending into place, the man started to drift backwards. He couldn't move but he could portray emotions through his eyes, they were screaming for help as tears started to form. He drew closer to the piping until it was touching his back, driving it upwards into his spine. The silence was split by his piercing scream, it was so loud and it sounded like a beast from hell. The pipe broke through the skin and still he was being dragged backwards. It could almost be seen pushing towards his chest then up his throat, the sound of screaming had been replaced by gurgling and crunching sounds.

The worker pinned to the wall tried as hard as he could to close his eyes, but a something was forcing them open. The man had slowed his drifting just for a moment before the silence was yet again broken by an ungodly sound, the sound of his skull cracking open. The pipe had busted his face open and splattered parts of his head across the hall. His blood had covered his coworker, some had even gotten in his mouth, who was now crying and begging for his life. The force holding him up had instantaneously let him down and he fell to his knees.

"Please… no…" He whimpered to the boy who was staring down the hall towards nothing. When suddenly the man's head jerked to the right and a series of cracks and pops could be heard. With his head turned unnaturally backwards, he dropped to the ground and the silence returned. Q continued forward this time leaving more than bloody footprints, but instead leaving bodies.

David and Vinny walk in silence, Vinny's anger clouding all judgment. David is first to break the silence.

"What's that?" he pointed at an opening ahead of them, a dim gloomy light was lighting up the area.

"Don't make a sound." Vinny hissed, worried that it was from the head of that creature. They silently creeped forward towards the opening; as they got closer a horrid smell overtook the area. David wretched as the smell became thick and horrible, it smelled like a truck of rotting meat. Then as they moved forward Vinny noticed a glint and dropped to his knees as David noticed the blood on the ground where Vinny looked.

"It can't be…" Vinny whimpered. David ignored this and walked forward, something felt different, this wasn't Jane's blood. Vinny's disbelief quickly turned to anger and he slowly stood up. David had gotten to the pool of blood, curiosity taking over his senses and blocking out the smell. He turned the corner and what he saw he couldn't comprehend; Vinny caught up and he too froze at what he saw.

Jane was floating in the middle of the room, suspended in air like a half filled balloon. There was other stuff too, the room itself look to be an underground library and on the ground right in front of them was the creature squashed like a bug. The vile thing was fleshy and rotten, it's legs were like a spider's and had little hairs sticking out randomly. Finally, standing directly behind Jane's floating body was Q, standing there with his bloodied owl in his hand. Suddenly a voice could be heard.

"I think you are finding my game of checkers quite entertaining aren't you?" The voice bellowed, it sounded familiar but it was not known. David thought for a second but upon hearing the word checkers, he knew exactly who it was.

"You liar! I thought you were Scott! You're just..."

"Let her go!" Vinny shouted, cutting David's words off. "Let her go now or I swear to god I will..."

The sounds of footsteps cut Vinny off and out of the shadows, Scott Reynolds stepped forward, his face lined with a wicked smile. Vinny Lunged forwards at him but he disappeared and suddenly he was standing behind Q with a peculiar black stone held to the boy's neck.

"Vinny! Stop or..."

Yet again Vinny ran after the sheriff, this time Scott raised his hand and brought the sharp stone quickly with such a force that it had cut straight into Q's stomach. They boy screamed in pain, in consequence Jane burst into nothing but flesh and blood at an instant. Vinny dropped to his knees and stared at the sight, he was speechless. Jane was gone in an instant and they could do nothing to change it. Vinny was devastated but this time David's rage grew. He was tired of the death, the games, the confusion, and he was tired of the stranger. David stepped towards the stranger who was disguised as the town sheriff, as he did the stone was yet again raised and stabbed into the boy, this time in the ribs. The boy yelped again and this time Vinny had burst into flesh and blood soaking David in gore from head to toe. Still David walked forward without words, anger drove him.

The stranger had thrown the boy to the ground who was now writhing in pain, bleeding out, and crying for his mother, not knowing why this was happening. As David drew nearer he came to a halt right in front of the stranger who held out the stone to David and smiled with his eerily thin mouth that stretched from ear to ear. David didn't even question it, he grabbed the stone and thrusted it towards his neck, splitting it open and splattering blood everywhere. Suddenly the cave started to melt, everything started spinning. David didn't bother to look around, he only stared into the Devil's eyes as the sound of an eerie giggle could be heard. Finally things went dark and David fell to the ground.

A knock could be heard, it had sounded like a door. David opened his eyes, he was lying down on his bed. The knock hit again, it was small and polite, as if it were trying not to disturb anyone. David sat up and groaned from exhaustion.

"Yeah?" He had managed to say while looking around in a daze.

"David? It's me. I made some tea." James' voice sounded like heaven compared to what he had just experienced. He was about to tell James to come in when he noticed a figure standing outside of the window, it had long hair. Other than the hair it had no distinct features and it had taken David by surprise. In response David yelped in fear causing James to quickly burst into the room.

"What? Are you okay? What is it?" James was very alarmed, but as David looked at James the figure had disappeared when he looked back.

"It's just… there was a… never mind." David rubbed his eyes, he must be seeing things from just waking up, still feeling the effects of that dream. James shrugged and sat on the bed, still worried, he set the tea on the bedside table and grabbed David's hand. He held David's hand with both of his rubbing his thumbs up and down the back and the front. A worried and caring look in his eyes.

"You've been asleep all day, so I buried her this morning over in the cemetery." his eyes were filled with sorrow and they were just staring at David's hand. In response David suddenly remembered what had happened. Kaitlyn was gone, she had died in the worst way possible. David hiccoughed and held his other hand up to his mouth staring off into space. James went silent and pulled David into his arms, holding him until the pain eased. They sat frozen like this for what felt like hours. Finally James broke the silence.

"Hey, your tea is gonna get cold." He smiled and said light heartedly "She is okay, she won't feel the pain anymore."

David let out a small sigh of relief that could be considered a little laugh.

"Okay well give me the tea so I can drink it." He said as he reached across James over to the table unable to reach the tea. James extended his arm out grabbed the tea, giving it to David's extended and empty hand. Taking a sip David sat up straight, he needed to tell James about his dream. They sat on the bed facing each other and spoke for hours about what had happened. What the dream meant and whether it was actually real or not. David could vividly remember the people he had met, the choices they made, and the conversations they had. Whether it was a dream or not, it would play a big role in what was to come.

13 PREPARATIONS FOR THE END

After several hours of conversing and figuring out what is happening, they heard a knock at the front door. David jumped because the town was still empty to their knowledge. Whatever it was knocking must be a trick or some kind of trap. James looked at David with a worried expression.

"Should we answer it?" James asked.

David, without answering him, got up and walked out of the bedroom and down the hall to the living room. James followed, preparing to hit something if they were to be attacked. The knock had been quiet and it happened almost a minute ago. David waited by the front door to see if there really was someone knocking. James stepped forward and looked through the peephole, seeing nobody there he turned to David and shrugged.

"Maybe we just imagined it, there was nobody there."

"We couldn't have both imag…" another knock at the door cut David off. This time the knock was louder and sounded persistent. James grabbed the handle and quickly opened the door, and to their surprise there had been nobody there; Instead, a box was sitting on the doormat with a paper placed carefully on the top. Without saying anything David grabbed the paper, opened it up, and began reading it.

"*As the town starts to fizzle, it seems to only have one hope. The Dazzling Duo, David Walker and his infamous sidekick James Haul… I hope that you like my gift, it seems to have swallowed something that could be useful to you in your endeavors. I anticipate that you will enjoy this, it will be fun to watch.* It's signed with a smile… I just want it to end…" David had finished reading the letter and took a deep breath.

James stepped forward and brought the box inside. They sat down on the couch and opened it together. They froze, staring into the box with wide eyes. Fear coursing through their veins, their sanity slowly being drained by these haunting events.

"Jane?" David managed to choke out this single word. Her head was placed inside the box, her eyes open and glazed. Her mouth was sewn shut and her hair was tangled and matted. There was not that much blood, but the absence of her body made their stomachs queasy. She had been mutilated and used. James just sat there stumped, then he reached into his pocket for his knife. David stopped him as he brought the knife up to her cold lips.

"Wait, how do we know this is real? She was in my dream…" He pondered for a second and then his need to know the truth overtook him; he took the knife from James and cut the stitches from her lips. When he cut the last stitch and set the knife down her jaw snapped open, as if it were spring locked. They both jumped at the sudden movement and then inspected the new scene. Inside of her mouth was a crystal, large enough that it filled the whole cavity. She was missing all of her teeth and it seemed as though her tongue was ripped from her throat.

David almost vomited and he looked away, James had picked up the knife and worked at prying the crystal out of her mouth. There were some horrible sucking and sloshing sounds until finally they heard a loud crack. James had broken her jaw but the crystal popped right out. The popping noise had caused David to run to the trashcan in the kitchen, vomiting as if his insides were rejecting his entire existence.

"There is something inside the crystal." James said as he took the box with her head inside to the trash outside. He didn't' want to see it anymore, let alone think about it. After he came back inside and David was done clearing his guts out, they sat at the couch with the crystal.

"Should we break it? I have a hammer." David coughed the words up as if it hurt to speak.

"Well there doesn't seem to be any other way of getting it out." James said as he fumbled around in his hands. David got up and opened a drawer in the kitchen, pulled out a small hammer, and brought it back to the living room where James held the crystal. As he walked into the room James set the crystal on the side table next to the couch; this was the only table that was still standing. David handed the hammer over and stood to watch as James lifted it up and brought in swinging down, smashing the crystal into little shards. There was piece of paper and a little grey stone laying where the crystal used to sit. James picked up the stone and started to examine it and then grabbed the slip of paper to read it.

"*Visus et cognitionis*, what do you think that means?" He asked handing the paper to David. As David took the paper the words shifted, the letters transformed, and suddenly it was English.

"Sight of Knowledge." David spoke aloud, he was able to read the words clearly as if he was fluent. "I don't know how I know that, but that's what it says."

"Oh, well what do you think it means? There was also a stone with it." James announced as he reached for the stone. Then suddenly the stone shifted away from his hand and he was startled by the sudden movement. When he reached for it again, the stone moved away, but this time it flew at David. Reflexes saved him from being hit in the face, he had caught the stone.

"What on earth…" David was cut off by a bright light that shone through his hands. James stood in confusion as he saw nothing happening. When David opened his palm the light was blinding and he could no longer see the room around him.

"David!" James yelled as David dropped the stone and collapsed to the floor.

As David opens his eyes he sees stars surrounding him. There is a platform beneath his feet but as far as he can see there is nothing else in view.

"Where am I..." He let out. He got up to his feet and tried to look around but the platform took off throwing him off balance. It was taking him somewhere. He looked down at the platform he was standing on and noticed something odd. It was a book, a large book that was the color of emptiness. There was writing on it but as David looked they seemed to shift from his vision leaving him unable to read the title. The book seemed to slow and a cloud formed to his right. In it a picture was created, people were in a cage made of stone. They laid unconscious in their prison, all except for one person, Conner.

"Conner!" screamed David as he tried to run towards the image, only to remember he was on a book in space, almost falling of the edge. As if reacting to his voice, the boy in the cloud looked up and reached for the bars imprisoning him. He looked directly at David, as if he could see him. Holding up his hand, Conner showed David his hand was covered in blood then he pointed to the ground. The image shifted and David was now looking at the floor of the prison where there was a painting made from blood. This painting was a map to the cave on the outskirts of town. The old mine.

David was suddenly lifted into the air and the cloud dissipated. He was being held in place above the book, where it opened up to a page in the middle. On this page were words so small that he couldn't make them out.

"REVELARE" a voice bellowed from seemingly nowhere. Suddenly the words shifted and created several pictures. They were symbols and directions. If David were to defeat the stranger, he would need to create these symbols from his blood while bellowing out these words 'ille qui damnatur nunquam revertitur.' The book closed and David was dropped back on to its cover. The same voice spoke again, this time louder than before. It felt almost as if it were in David's head.

"The blood will spill! It will be consumed! The portal will open! Death will reign!" With the resounding echo of this voice, David jolted back to reality. He was lying on the floor with James shaking his shoulders.

"David?! What happened?" James was almost in tears. "You fell to the ground as soon as the stone touched you and then you wouldn't respond... You stopped breathing..." He hiccoughed. David looked at James confused, then jumped to his feet when he realized what happened.

"I know how to kill it" David said wide eyed.

14 REVELATION

The truck pulled up to a rolling stop as David and James neared the edge of town where there was a closed off road to the old mine. They have to walk almost a mile up the overgrown dirt path to make it to the entrance. David gets out of the truck making no sound and James follows suit. Reaching under the seats to grab some tools for weapons they hear a chattering sound, David looks up to see what it is and he sees something that he wished he could erase. Melody was sitting in a branch, but it wasn't her, she has been morphed into something terrible.

"Mel? What happened to you?" David said staring at this monstrosity. Suddenly she made a terrible sound, as if all of her bones were cracking and her back was splitting open. A pair of boney and bloody wings sprung out of her spine, stretching out as far as they could reach. Melody let out a horrible screech that sounded like a human in agony, this was no longer David's cat. It suddenly flew towards the truck at them with insane speed and precision but before David could even react the creature flew face first into a crowbar. James had stopped the creature in its tracks. "What the heck just happened?" David yelled.

James didn't speak, he just turned to David and grinned.

"I bet you are wondering what happened to Mr. Haul now, aren't you?" The voice coming from James was not his own. It was low and gravely, almost chilling. "It isn't time for your blood to spill so it was only natural for me to stop your irritating cat. She couldn't wait for my orders. Let's see how your boy toy succeeds in obedience, shall we?"

David froze, he was so filled with anger that he could move. He only spoke in a calm yet rage induced voice.

"I don't know what your plans are, but you will leave this place or I will personally kill you myself." David had never spoke in this tone before but it's all he could do.

"Don't fret, I know *exactly* what you will do. You will smile!" The stranger replied as James' body started to morph into something inhuman and disgusting. His body grew in size, ripping his clothes to shreds. All of his limbs twisted and snapped in unnatural positions, they seemed to be oozing blood and other substances or of its pores. His glasses fell to the ground as his face melted and became misshapen. The small grin that he had before grew from ear to ear, with saliva dripping from his unholy teeth.

Suddenly the stranger was standing before David in his true form, he looked so unholy, an abomination to earth. David's eyes lifted to stare at the beast face to face.

"I do not fear you!" He said as loud as he could to show his strength.

"I hoped you would say that." the demons voice was almost incomprehensible, it sounded as though his voice was shredded. Then the abomination jumped into the air and disappeared from sight.

David walked forward and bent down to the ground, picking up James' glasses.

"I promise I will fix this…" David said quietly to the glasses. "We'll even go to the burger joint after all of this is over." a single tear fell from his left eye. Standing back up, David wiped away his tear and with that he also wiped away any fears he had going forward.

David turned to look at deformed fiend who was now lying on the ground perfectly still. He picked Melody up and laid her in the seat of his truck the closed the doors to find the cave. Walking over to where the path was, he stood for a moment staring down the path. His nerves were increasing by the minute, what seemed to be the end was coming closer and closer but there were still so many unanswered questions.

With a large breathe he took his first step towards the end on his own. If he failed, he would lose his whole town, his family, everything he had ever cared about. As he walked down the path, thoughts raced through his mind and he had failed to notice that he was being followed.

David slowed as he eventually felt as if something was watching him. Asking who was there, he had turned around to face the path behind him.

"David?" a small voice let out from behind one of the trees. The voice sounded familiar, it was Q. the small boy stepped out onto the path, he looked rough and beaten.

"Q? but how are you here? You were in my dream, you were…" David was stunned, but this wasn't the strangest event to have happened to him.

"I have to help you, otherwise you will only do what he wants." Q said, taking a step forward. David hesitated, not knowing if he could trust Q after what happened to James. He decided that he would trust Q at least for now.

"Alright well what do we do now then?" Right as the words left David's mouth a twig snapped ahead of them. Out of the shadows a beast stepped forward, snarling. Q stepped ahead of David and lifted his hand. A vibrating sound filled David's head and suddenly the beast was lifted into the air and brought towards them. It looked like Brutus but its teeth were overgrown and it had no skin on left on its muzzle. His limbs were deformed, they looked almost like a human's on all fours. Brutus had little to no fur left and he was thrashing around in air. He looked distressed and angry but looking into his eyes there was only sadness and regret.

"These fabricated beasts were made by him and they were meant to be pieces used in this unholy game of checkers. You were meant to kill them because they were Alderton's pets. I am here to change that." Q cocked his head and Brutus suddenly started to transform, his limbs and teeth shrank back to normal size and his hair rapidly grew back. Q had turned the dog back into himself. With the ceasing of movement, Q let the dog down and he was now lying unconscious on the ground.

"Why is he using them… " David questioned "and why do you know so much?" Q walked forward, forcing David to move along with him.

"The stranger is a true stranger to this world I guess you could say. You see, I am not of this world either, but I have been trapped here and I lost all recollection of any previous life that I had." Q yet again sounded very mature for the child that he was. David began to realize that there was much more to this that he once thought.

"So if you're not Q, then who are you?" David asked as they slowly walked along the path.

"My name is Quincy Ashur, I am still the same person that you originally met. I was imprisoned there by Ludos, the stranger you seek to defeat. Ludos wiped my memory and decided to mess with your mind. He is a cruel games man." Q started to scratch his head. "I still don't understand why I am involved, it may just be to give you a fighting chance."

"So this is all just a game to him, this Ludos guy?" David rubbed his chin, trying to comprehend everything. "But why me? Why Alderton?" Quincy stopped in his tracks, they arrived at the mine entrance.

David felt a sudden pang of dread in his stomach, something was wrong. Suddenly a loud scream erupted from inside the mine.

It was Conner.

15 THE END?

David took off running into the cave, he didn't give it a second thought. Conner was in danger and he would stop at nothing to save his brother. Q ran after him and they entered the unlit cave. It was very dark once inside, luckily it was a straight shot down the mine for a while, so they just walked along the edge for guidance. After the initial scream it had gone silent. Absolutely no sound and David started to worry about what had happened to Conner.

Finally they spotted a dim light farther down the tunnel. It seemed to be coming from a large room at the end. The dread inside David worsened as they inched closer to the light, what would he find? Could he really stop Ludos and save the town? As they arrived at the entrance to the room with the light, they noticed shadow on the wall. It had three arms, two on the left and one on the right. It had two legs of different lengths and a large head. The creature seemed to be pacing back and forth in wait. David stepped on a small rock and a crackling sound was made under his foot.

The shadow of the creature came to a sudden halt and waited in the spot silently. David covered his mouth in attempt to be silent. The creature let out a sound that made David and Q gasp. The sound was a terrible scream, it sounded like Conner and James both; it had their voices. The shadow started to move again, it was leaving. The two sat and waited for the creature to be gone before making even the smallest noise. After what felt like thirty minutes they decided to look into the area and see what was there. David walked around the corner first then Q followed.

It was a large cavern and in the center of the room was a pile of rocks that left off an orange glow, bright enough to fill the entire room with light. There were strange symbols written all around on the walls. On the opposite side of the cavern was a section that was closed off by a bunch of rusty bars. Multiple cages were placed in piles around the large bars, they held many different creatures. Every creature deformed and disgusting, just as Melody and Brutus. David walked towards the cages and saw that on the other side of the bars was all of the towns people. They were unconscious and lying about in the prison. He noticed a familiar face laying with them, Vinny. He was unconscious but he seemed to still have an angry face. Q had walked towards the glowing rocks, picking one up then quickly dropping it.

"Hot!" he let out as he shook the pain off of his hand.

"Hey Q, we gotta get them out of here. Can you bend the bars with your mind or something?" David questioned inspecting the rusty metal. Then Q looked over at the bars and pointed at something.

"Or you could just open the door to the cage…" He said almost laughing. David looked embarrassed but he walked over and opened the door.

"David lookout!" Q yelled, but before david could react a hand grabbed his shoulder from behind and threw him back several feet.

When David looked up at what threw him, he saw a creature that had three arms, two on the left and one on the right. The creature had come back. Q had tried to lift it the same way he had lifted Brutus but it was holding a large piece of wood and threw it at Q, knocking him unconscious. David could only stare at the beast, it looked as if two people were sewn together and made into a monster. Those two people were Conner and James.

"I'M SORRY" it had let out. Though it was a raspy sound, James and Conner could both clearly be heard. "HELP?" it seemed as though it didn't want to hurt David at all in fact it wanted to help him. David sat there unable to speak or move. Suddenly the creature turned to the townspeople and started sadly for a moment. Then he let out that same horrible scream from earlier. The beast was trying to wake them up but he couldn't. David relaxed, knowing that the creature meant no harm but he was still tense because it looked like Conner and James. He stood up and stepped nearer to the cages. He reached out to grab a bar when he winced. David had forgotten about his arm being wrapped up, it must have split back open when he was thrown back.

Blood dripped from his arm and the creature snapped around and looked directly at David's arm. Before David could react, he was being held by his arm over the beast with its mouth wide open trying to catch any bloody drops. David let out a yelp and a single drop fell from his arm and landed on the creature's tongue. Suddenly it dropped David and its body began to bubble and transform. David reeled back and crawled towards Q waking him up.

"What's happening?" Q let out opening his eyes and noticing the creature. They both stared in awe as it began to flash and pulse, until finally it became too bright to look at. They squeezed their eyes shut and opened them once the light dimmed again. In the creature's spot were two people, Conner and James. They looked weak and tired, like they had just woken up from a long nap. David quickly got up to run over to them but his arm leaked blood onto the floor, hitting one of the symbols in a circle around the pile of glowing rocks. Every symbol in the cavern suddenly lit up as if they were turned on by a light switch.

Out of nowhere the cave started rattling and all of the townspeople started to wake up and shuffle about in the prison. The cavern seemed as if it were about to crumble and cave in, the now wakened people started to panic and run out of the room to the exit of the mine. Only four people were left in the room, Q, Conner, James, and David.

They all huddled close together, something was coming and it was not good. The pile of glowing stones suddenly fell into the ground as a hole was opening underneath of it. The room was instantly filled with an almost unbearable heat. In the center of the room was a hole that flames seemed to erupt out of. All of the caged creatures suddenly went insane and bashed at their doors, they were trying to escape. As they were distracted by the creatures in the cages a voice sounded that filled the entire cave.

"David Walker! It is time!" At the sound if the voice every creature went silent and still. The group turned to look back at the hole in the center of the room and instead of a hole was a hideous, smiling demon. Ludos.

Q suddenly dropped to the ground unconscious.

"Oh, poor thing. His kind is to far under me and they cant handle my presence." The demon let out a horrible laugh that sent shivers down their spines. Conner tried to run towards the entrance but the demon cut him off, he was sent flying through the cave and he landed hard against the wall and coughed up some blood.

"Conner!" David yelled and tried to run towards his younger brother. He was suddenly lifted into the air by an unseen force and no longer able to move.

"Fool, your blood has released me. You fell right into my little trap. Did you really think that vision of the book and your brother was showing you how to stop me? It was how to summon me at full strength!" The demon cackled loudly as he spoke.

"But that... voice... it couldn't... have been yours..." David choked out. This surprised the demon.

"What voice?" David was thrown to the ground and James ran to him to help him up. "Do not lie to me boy! I will make your life a living hell." With that the demon raised his twisted arm above his head preparing to smash the two when David suddenly stood up.

"My life is already a living hell!" he bellowed. Suddenly David remembered what the voice had said. *Blood will spill. It will be consumed!* He lifted his arm that was bleeding and shouted four words. "It will be consumed!" he suddenly threw his arm into his mouth and began to drink his own blood.

The demon waited patiently as nothing happened, James stepped back wondering what might happen. The demon laughed hard when nothing happened.

"Idiot, what would drinking your own blood do to affect me?" This gave David and James an idea. "Now I am going to start killing everything you love! ONE BY…" The demon stopped when he notice that James had drank some of David's blood too.

James' eyes began to emanate light and all the creatures in the cages went wild yet again. The demon took a step back as James produce more light that became almost blinding. James took a step forward and lifted his hand towards the demon and a beam of light shone from his hand that was so bright that the demon began to boil.

"Ut malediceret David Walker…" Ludos tried to speak but he was forced to retreat back into the hole and it closed up behind him. Suddenly the entire cave flashed brightly. They were forced to cover their eyes by the brightness. When it had finally dimmed all of the cages were gone, the glowing stones were replaced by a lantern, and James was laying on the ground unconscious.

Conner and Q both regained consciousness and walked over to David. Conner looked exhausted and Q didn't remember anything after Ludos showed up.

"Let's go home…" David said picking James up off of the ground. They left the cave, fully intact. They had a few bumps and bruises but they all survived. When they arrived at David's truck, a grey tabby leaned on the window to great them.

"Melody?" David was astounded that she was back to normal. They all hopped in the truck and began the drive back into town. The sun was just coming up, it was dawn. The ride back was mostly silent except for the sounds of an occasional meow and the sputtering engine. They had driven past the playground and line of trees. They drove past the coffee shop and the bookstore. Everything seemed completely normal, shop owners and farmers were up and starting the town for the day. The people all seemed to be back to normal. They had done it, they defeated Ludos. David could finally relax, though he was still haunted by many unanswered questions that he may never find the answer to.

EPILOGUE

The town seemed relatively back to normal, none of the townspeople remembered the events of the previous day. There were still some people and pets missing, there have been missing persons posters put up all over town. David and the others remembered the whole thing. Q stayed with David, seeing as he had nowhere else to go and he wasn't from this world. James, Conner, and Q all helped David clean up the house over the next few days. As David was cleaning he noticed a piece of paper under some rubble. It was a letter addressed to David, he read it out loud to the others.

David,

I have been taken. That creature that I saw take my dog broke in while we slept that night, it spoke to me in a language i have never heard and then it changed. It changed into me! It told me to write you a note , telling you that i've been kidnapped. It said that the only way to find me is to confront the past that you never completed. I think it is talking about when you went to college? Please help me… I'm scared…

- *Kaitlyn Lambers*

TAKE A LOOK AT BOOK 2

TEASER

David climbed up onto the altar after Rachel, they were soon followed by James and Q. The altar had a vent-like structure under each of them and a handle sticking out above each opening. Rachel looked at David, worried for what would happen next. She grabbed her handle, David felt he should do the same.

"Are you sure about this? What will happen if it isn't me?" David said his voice stuttering. Rachel gave him a halfhearted smile then looked back at the altar. Her body began to pulse, it was as if something was flowing through her. Q and James quickly stepped off the altar in fear, then she stood completely still. She seemed almost lifeless.

"Iudicium dat semita!" Rachel bellowed out with her eyes rolled back and her head tilted forwards. She jerked her head to look at David, yet this didn't feel like Rachel staring at him.

"Grab the handle!" she hissed. He felt compelled to follow her directions and he grabbed the handle. His hand was straining as it felt great pain, the burning sensation started to spread to his forearm and it started to glow as well. The glowing started to focus to one spot on is arm and formed a ring around it; the ring never quite met in the middle but formed a pattern around itself. When the burning started to cease, so too did the glowing light. Q and James just stood there watching, not knowing if this were a good or bad thing.

Rachel suddenly dropped from her spot and landed on the floor, she was unconscious. David leapt down to help her and the glowing lights instantly dimmed, she laid there mumbling to herself as the boys all ran to her.

"Did it work?" she asked weakly.

"I don't know, how can we tell?" David replied, forgetting about what had just happened.

"Your arm! It worked!" She yelled.

www.ingramcontent.com/pod-product-compliance
Lightning Source LLC
Chambersburg PA
CBHW021926170626
46807CB00007B/2999